Peppa Pig™

Peppa's New Neighbours

Daddy Pig is working hard.
He is building a new house.

The new house looks
very small.
"Is it a house for elves
and fairies?" asks Peppa.
"No," chuckles Daddy Pig.
"This is just a model."

Daddy Pig shows
Peppa and George
a drawing of what
the real house
will look like.

"Something is missing!"
says Peppa.

She draws a swing to go
outside the house.
"Perfect!" decides
Daddy Pig.

Daddy Pig takes Peppa and
George to see the new house.

Brrrm!

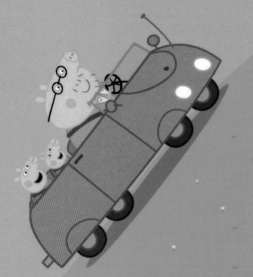

"Here we are!" he snorts.
"But Daddy," says Peppa,
"there's nothing here!"

Chug!
Chug!

"That's because the building work hasn't started yet!" replies Daddy Pig.

Mr Bull is going to build the
new house for Daddy Pig.
"Can you build it
exactly like this please?"
says Daddy Pig.

"But bigger,"
adds Peppa.

Mr Bull shouts to his friends.
"Mr Pig wants a house!"
"Is it going to be built of straw?"
asks Mr Rhino.

"Or sticks?" asks Mr Labrador.
"Or bricks?" asks Mr Bull.

Daddy Pig wants the
new house to be made
out of bricks.

Mr Bull gets straight to work.
"Can we help?" wonders Peppa.
"You can lay the first brick," smiles Mr Bull.
Mr Bull tells George to put a blob of mortar
on the ground. Mortar is a special kind of mud
that sticks bricks together.

Grunt!

Grunt!

Each brick must be laid
straight and level.
It takes ages.
"Will you finish it
today?" asks Peppa.
"You can't build a house
in a day!" snorts Mr Bull.
"It will be finished . . .
tomorrow."

The next morning, Peppa and George go
straight over to see the new house.
"It's finished!" snorts Peppa.
"It's almost finished!" says Daddy Pig.
"It just needs to be inspected."

Mr Rabbit is the building inspector.
He looks carefully at the new house.
"Very good," he decides, "but you forgot the swing!"

"Oh no we
didn't!" shouts
Mr Bull.

The house is all ready for the new neighbours
to move in. Mr Wolf and his family arrive.

Mr Wolf tries huffing and puffing, but the house doesn't fall down. It is very strong.

"What is the new house made of?" asks Mr Wolf.

"Bricks," replies Daddy Pig, "so don't even think about it."

Wendy Wolf likes the new swing.
"Can you push me?" asks Peppa.
"No," grins Wendy. "I'll huff and puff you instead!"

Hee!
Hee!

had to fly at last!

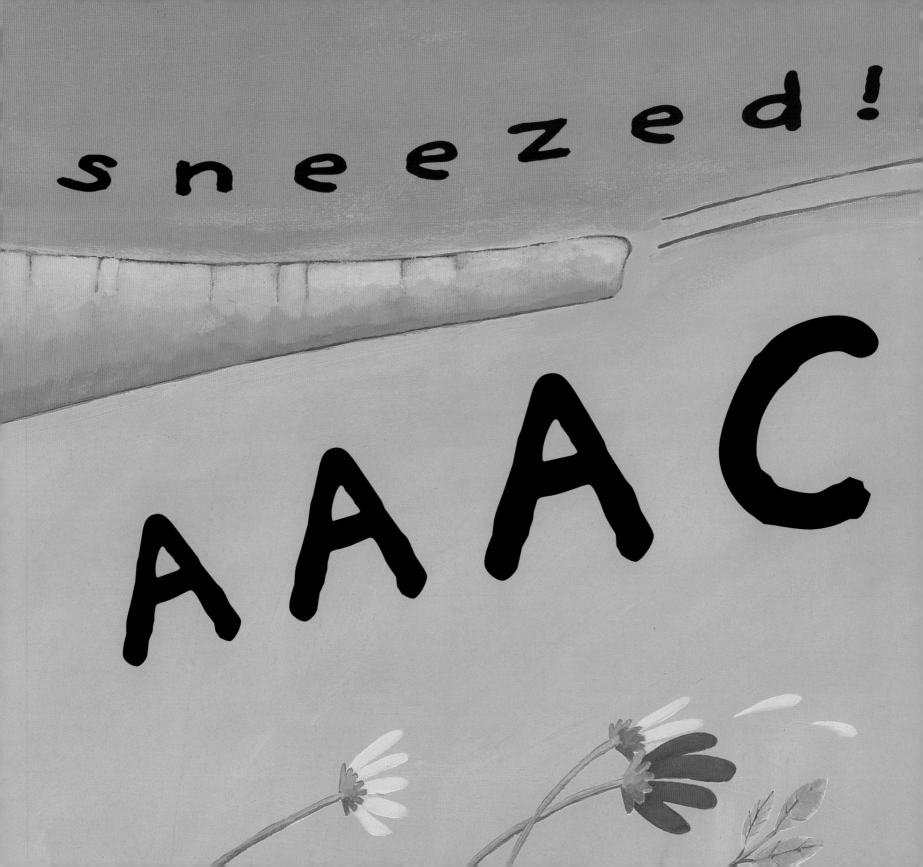

H O o o

and poor old lazy ladybird . . .